Cat
UP A TREE

A Story in Poems

by Anne Isaacs
illustrated by Stephen Mackey

DUTTON CHILDREN'S BOOKS ◆ NEW YORK

With special thanks to my editor, Donna Brooks—A.I.

Text copyright © 1998 by Anne Isaacs
Illustrations copyright © 1998 by Stephen Mackey, LIP International
All rights reserved. Published in the United States 1998 by Dutton Children's Books,
a member of Penguin Putnam Inc. 375 Hudson Street, New York, New York 10014
Designed by Sara Reynolds • Printed in Italy
First Edition • 10 9 8 7 6 5 4 3 2 1

Library of Congress Cataloging-in-Publication Data
Isaacs, Anne. Cat up a tree / by Anne Isaacs; illustrated by Stephen Mackey.—1st ed. p. cm.
Summary: A series of poems describe the reactions of various characters—from a young girl
and her father to a fireman, to a robin, to the cat itself—when a cat climbs a tree.
ISBN 0-525-45994-4 (hc) 1. Cats—Juvenile poetry. 2. Children's poetry, American. [1. Cats—Poetry.
2. American poetry.] I. Mackey, Stephen, ill. II. Title.
PS3559.S12C38 1998 811'.54—DC21 98-10130 CIP AC

For Sam, with love
A.I.

For Elliot, Esmé & Helen
S.M.

Contents

Invitation

Suppose the cat had lingered on the ground
Or climbed unseen, another place or time.
There'd be no tale. But high among the leaves
A robin cried; the cat began to climb.

The girl would not have given chase,
Nor fireman or father joined the fray;
All that followed would be different
Had the cat not climbed a tree that day.

Is spring the trickster who conspires
To summon life from earth to branches?
Don't stop to ask, "What happens once I'm there?"
Come among the leaves and take your chances.

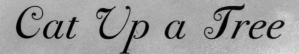

Cat Up a Tree

GIRL: Come and see! There's a cat up a tree!
  Let's take him home as a pet!
FATHER: Don't be misled by the semblance of charm;
  What you see may not be what you get.

GIRL: Oh, but *this* cat will nap curled up on my lap
  As harmless and calm as a yawn.
FATHER: Or tear up the house in search of a mouse!
  I'll be screeched out of bed before dawn.

GIRL: There aren't many pets whose needs are so few—
  Just milk and some yarn in a ball.
FATHER: Unless they've a preference for caviar and silk.
  Who's going to pay for it all?

GIRL: You ought to be grateful I've chosen this cat;
  I *could* choose a scorpion or snake.
FATHER: Where are you going? Come back here this minute!
  You're making a major mistake.

GIRL: I'll go find the fireman. *He'll* get me the cat!
  I'll ask for the cat-catcher, too.
FATHER: Slow down! Reconsider—I'll buy you a turtle!
  Some goldfish! A long-tailed shrew!

The Secret Life of a Cat

Embers in the palm of night
Light my way through tangled grasses;
I await the rising moment,
Wary of each wind that passes.

Keeping watch amid the shadows
Silent by the water hole;
Every inward flare of tumult
Frozen in a fierce control.

Life-breath whispers all around me,
Trembles every stem and vine;
Winged with fear, gazelles will scatter:
Africa is mine.

The Fireman's Lament

You can't catch a cat with a ladder or rope,
A dishful of fish or a hatful of hope.
Forget the net: it will all come to naught
Unless the cat should decide to be caught.

Take it from me: I've put in my share
Of bone-numbing hours thirty feet in the air,
Dreaming of home and a hot mug of tea
While casting for shadows on top of a tree.

A cat is a sorcerer. He'll purr and look gentle—
Beware not to weaken or get sentimental.
He knows that he's won, once you're pinned by his stare;
He'll vanish—like that! without trace, in midair.

I'd rather face flames raging out of control
Than a cat, who's a fire with four legs and a soul.
Still, I wait on my ladder and take off my hat
To the prince of lost spaces, the uncatchable cat.

From the Notebook of a Cat-Catcher

ITEM: *Feline Anatomy*

Half a pound of water,
Quarter-pound of fur,
Seven ounces teeth and claws,
Two of purr.

ITEM: *Shopping List*

Trout heads, carp tails,
Assorted dregs and slops;
Anything the fisherman
Or butcher drops.

ITEM: *The Personality of a Cat*

Conceited, fickle,
Aloof, imperious,
Unnerving, undeserving,
Confoundingly mysterious.

ITEM: *Skills Required for the Job of Cat-Catcher*

The muscle, wit, and nerve
Of a dozen samurai;
Clairvoyance, tightrope training,
Or ability to fly.

The Robin's Cry

Danger! Hide! A cat is coming!
Swiftly! Flee! He's drawing near!
Like a storm cloud, creeping closer,
Omen-heavy, dark as fear.

Can he see my newborn nestlings?
Sound a warning! Scatter! Fly!
Hurry! Lead him off! Distract him!
May is not the month to die.

Cat! I call you from the branches:
This way! Chase me! Climb! Pursue!
I cannot fly; my wing is broken.
Look: I hold it out to you.

Of my earliest life I just recall
A smoky kitchen, stone-tiled hall.
I drank from silver plates of milk
On firelit rugs of damask silk.

In my second life I sailed the seas
As cook's mate on the *Summer Breeze*.
Amid the swells I'd boil and bake
Catnip tea and catfish cake.

The Cat Reviews His First Four Lives

Mouse-scourge, bane of rat;
The third life I grew sly and fat.
My mission: keep the granary free
Of all who lurk or prowl—but me.

My fourth and favorite avocation,
I served a poet's inspiration.
(I say it in all modesty—)
Who better fit for Muse than me?

I've five more chances unredeemed
To live what I have only dreamed.
Perhaps I'll journey dale and dune
Along the lightpath of the moon,

Or set a queen with golden hair
To frighten mice beneath my chair,
Or, hoarse from hearthrug oratory,
Tell my grandkits one more story.

I'll tell them that I don't repent;
All my lives have been well spent.
And—keeping clear of dogs and rain—
I'd gladly live them all again.

Song of the Balloon Lady

Wayfarers in worlds apart,
Guided by a common star.
I a woman, you a cat;
In spirit, how alike we are.

You have taught me well and wisely:
How to call the sun to warm;
How to baffle those who'd tame us;
Conjure shelter in a storm.

I will look for you tomorrow,
Light of heart and light of load.
Lives await us, bright with promise,
Past the turnings of the road.

Praise for sun which daily cheers us;
Praise for stars which nightly guide;
Praise for paths which beckon onward;
And friends to travel by my side.

Wayfarers in worlds apart,
Guided by a common star.
I a woman, you a cat;
In spirit, how alike we are.

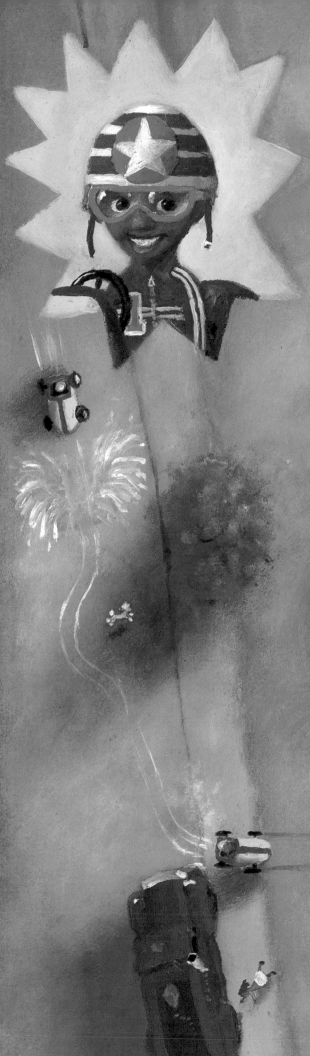

Box-Car Racer

At the top of High

Street:

I buckle my helmet, spit out my gum

Check the brakesropesteeringwheelaxletires

with one foot holding the box-

car

   over the

         edge

Then I push–off–and–jump–in allatonce

and we go!

No(?)where

(I get out and scrape the gum off the tire)

Once again:

       k-thock

       k-thock grrutcha

       grrutcha grrutcha jickety

       jickety jackety jickety jackety

>BLASTOFF<

Wings on my wheels

     jickety jackety

Fire in my feet

     jickety jackety—look out!

               Puddle: *whoosh*

               Poodle: whoa!

Nothing's gonna stop—

MAYDAY! FIRE TRUCK!

hard left! hard left!

jickety jackety

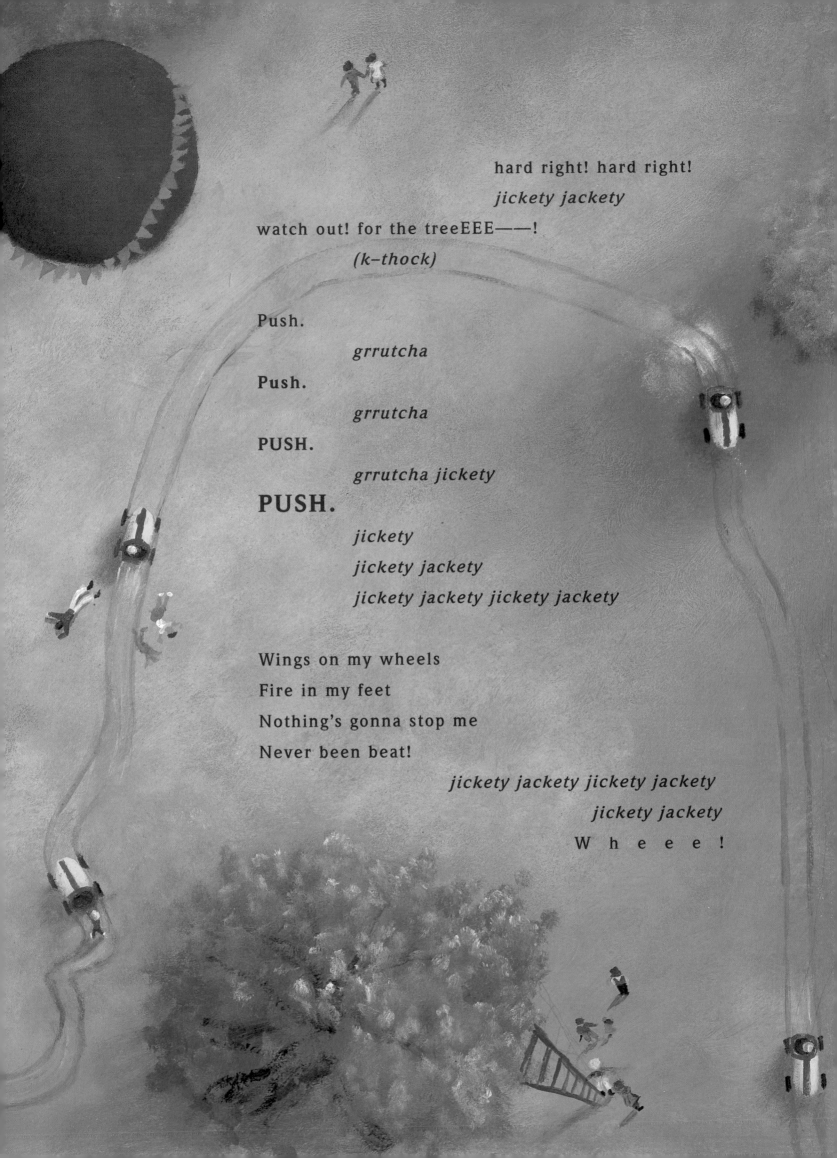

hard right! hard right!
jickety jackety

watch out! for the treeEEE——!
(k–thock)

Push.

      grrutcha

Push.

      grrutcha

PUSH.

      grrutcha jickety

PUSH.

      jickety
      jickety jackety
      jickety jackety jickety jackety

Wings on my wheels
Fire in my feet
Nothing's gonna stop me
Never been beat!

      jickety jackety jickety jackety
        jickety jackety
        W h e e e !

The Tree's Complaint

A plague upon the race of cats
Who scratch along my noble height,
Those caterwauling, mouse-breath brats
(Till they look down and scream in fright!)

Why all this fuss about a cat?
Does he weave boughs to bind together
Earth and sky? Or stand outdoors
To shelter you in stormy weather?

Would he let lightning strike him down
To keep you safe? Let axes hack
His limbs to bits, to warm your hearth?
Or let you rest upon his back?

Is it a cat who hangs the leaves
In scarlet banners from the sky,
Charms blossoms out of sticks,
Then floats them down as you walk by?

When in memory did a cat
Produce an apple, plum, or peach,
Perfume the air, or offer you
The only shade upon a beach?

No laurels grown upon *these* limbs
Will crown a cat's celebrity!
I long to see the day return
When poets sing in praise of *me*.

Night Rising

Ancient alchemist, wake! Arise:
Flood each echoing well with beams;
Scatter coins across the sky;
Pour down your cold, transmuting fire.

Constrained to the reach of branch and bone,
I'll bathe in your pure bright spell;
Then venture among the spheres, alone,
And leap like a comet, star to star.

I'll summon the crowd (who will gasp and cheer)
While I whirl a galactic jig:
The May Moon shines but once a year;
Follow and take a turn!

Like moonflowers, open as you climb
Till you grasp both leaves and stars!
So have I done, past moonlit times;
So I will do once more.

Moon Solitary

Who seeks to climb beyond his range
By setting foot to moss-grown themes?
What! No rhymes for 'orbiting dust heap'?
Enough! You praise me past all compass.

I've stared unblinking ages
At the sapphire blaze of earth
And never known its heat.
I'm but a bright loiterer, pocked secondary;
Such cosmic nothingness
A shadow may devour me entire.

I'd trade an eon of these weary rounds
To feel, just once, what I call forth—
A seething tide, to pull me from the strand,
Then fling me to the cold salt crest;
I'd join the sublunary fellowship
Of lovers, madmen,
Owls, dogs, and secret thrush,
Who wrestle poems from empty wind
And visions from the shore of night.

I'd rather set my heart aflame
And sing one hour in the self-born light
Than for all eternity reflect another's fire.

Out on a Limb

"What these citizens need," said the mayor,
Ascending without hesitation,
"Is a man with the leadership know-how
To take charge of this operation."

"Be careful!" the mayor commanded.
"One branch at a time, now; steady!"
The father felt giddy. He fretted
They had climbed high enough already.

The fireman clambered up next,
With the cat-catcher following him;
Then the bird and the girl quickly joined
All the rest in a row on the limb.

"It's going to rain," puffed the mayor.
"My joints are beginning to ache."
The father expressed misgivings;
He feared that the branch might break.

"It's twenty past eight," sighed the fireman.
"It will soon be too dark to see."
The father went pale at the prospect
Of spending the night in a tree.

Said the mayor, "Let's form a committee
To determine the fate of this cat."
"I've a book," said the cat-catcher stiffly,
"With rules precisely for that."

"But all the cat needs," cried the girl,
"Is someone to give him a home."
"On a glacier," the bird added quickly,
"On a peak in Tibet or Nome."

While they debated the matter,
The cat crept, unseen and alone,
Then lightly descended the branches
To follow a path of his own.

Going Home

I'll build a treehouse roofed with stars,
With spreading clouds for beams!

What will become of the cat on this earth
Where nothing is quite as it seems?

There was a time, I remember,
When I used to go at night,
As the round moon led a silver dawn
And the rose-glad wind blew white;
Down a branch from the casement
To a treewise company
Of cricketsong and sudden wings
And a frog's soliloquy.

Here's a pitcher of cream and plenty of tea;
Here's herring for company, cookies for me.
Oh, you can't catch a cat, but whatever you do,
In the space of a whisker a cat may catch you.

ITEM: *Strange Symptoms*
Heart: fluttery. Voice: gone.
Palms, both: cold and wet.
Brain: fogged in since 9:15
When I landed in his net.

The Cat Has the Last Word

If you'd learn the way of cats,
Heed what I advise:
Always land upon your feet;
Carry the moon in your eyes.